READING CHAMPION

Samir's
Best Sports Day

by Elizabeth Dale and Art Gus

W

Samir was excited. It was Sports Day at school and he really, really wanted to win a race. But he wasn't sure he was good enough. He never won anything at Sports Day.

3

Samir lined up with other children at the start of the egg and spoon race, clutching his spoon tightly. The egg wobbled on the spoon.

He was worried that it would fall off as soon as

he started running. He looked over at his mum.

She smiled at him and gave him a thumbs-up.

He felt a bit better.

When Mr Simms blew the whistle,

Samir started running.

But almost at once he dropped the egg.

Samir picked it up quickly and carried on.

But he dropped the egg again and he was

the last to cross the line. He was very upset.

"Never mind, Samir," said Mr Simms.

"You tried hard."

Next it was the high jump. Samir gazed at the bar. It seemed very high.

Samir watched as Izzy jumped over it.

But when Samir jumped, he knocked off the bar.

Afterwards, Samir clapped
as the other children jumped over the bar.

"Maybe I'll win this race?" thought Samir
as he lined up for the dressing up race.
After all, he was good at getting dressed
quickly. He did it every morning.

Mr Simms had put lots of dressing up clothes
on the track. As soon as the whistle went,
Samir ran to the big floppy hat and put it on.
Then he put on the baggy trousers. But he was
in such a rush that he didn't do up the button.

He hadn't got far when the trousers fell down and tripped him up.

Samir got up and ran again, holding his trousers. But he could not catch up.

Everyone clapped when he came last.

But Samir could not smile.

Mr Simms did not like to see Samir look sad.

"Well done for trying, Samir," said Mr Simms.

"Now, can you help me, please?

I need someone to take some photos of today

for our school newsletter and website.

Could you do that for me?"

Samir looked a bit worried. "I can try," he said.

Samir loved taking the photos.

He took one of Anna doing a very long jump.

Then it was the running race. Samir planned

to take a photo of the winner crossing the line.

But just as Mr Simms blew his whistle, Samir realised he was at the starting line, not the finishing line.

He ran as fast as he could to the finishing line and just managed to take a photo of Max crossing the line ahead of the others.

Samir was surprised when Mr Simms gave him
a gold winner's sticker.

"Well done, Samir," Mr Simms said. "You were
at the start when the whistle went and you were
first to cross the line. So you were the fastest."

Samir smiled. He had won a race, just like
he wanted. The crowd cheered and clapped –
and his mum cheered loudest of all.

Samir wore his gold sticker proudly as he took more photos. He took a photo of Lucy laughing as she threw her javelin backwards by mistake.

He took a photo of Simon making a funny face as he wobbled on his stilts and fell off.

He took a photo of Lisa giggling when she tripped up in the sack race.

None of them won a race or were given

a gold sticker. But they were all having fun.

And as he took their photos, Samir realised that

having fun was what mattered most of all.

It was his best Sports Day ever!

Story order

Look at these 5 pictures and captions.
Put the pictures in the right order
to retell the story.

1

Samir came last in the egg and spoon race.

2

Samir came first in the running race.